D1616830

ABOVE THE CLOUDS

WHAT REALLY HAPPENS IN HEAVEN DURING A THUNDERSTORM

WRITTEN BY STEPHANIE BARTON, CARLEY BARTON, AND SUE MILON

ILLUSTRATED BY KELLY MENGARELLI

Published by Many Seasons Press | 2020 | Mesa, Arizona

FIRST EDITION

ABOVE THE CLOUDS

What Really Happens in Heaven During a Thunderstorm

Copyright © 2020 by Stephanie Barton, Carley Barton, and Sue Milon

Illustrated by Kelly Mengarelli

Published by Many Seasons Press
(An Imprint of MultimediaPublishingProject.com)
PO Box 50553
Mesa, AZ 85208
480.939.9689 | ManySeasonsPress.com

Library of Congress Control Number: 2020916937

Paperback ISBN 13: 978-1-936885-37-4
Hardback ISBN 13: 978-1-936885-40-4

Printed in the United States of America.

To my amazing husband, Jay, for always being by my side and believing in me when I had this crazy idea to write a book. To my daughter, Carley, and son, Reece ~ know anything is possible when you set your mind to it. Thank you to my parents for always letting the three of us kids sleep on the floor next to your bed when we were scared during a thunderstorm.
– *Stephanie Barton*

To my loving family who always has my back.
– *Carley Barton*

To Grammie for instilling in me the love of reading and to Pa for enchanting Bon, Rob, Doug and me with his amazing stories of Archibald and Blackbeard the Pirate.
– *Sue Milon*

On a dark and stormy night,

a loud clap of thunder woke Grace up

and she cried out for her mommy.

"It's all right, Grace,"

said her mommy.

"It might be scary for you, but let me tell you

about the incredible party going on

above the clouds

in heaven."

Above the clouds,

the angels in heaven are having

an amazing dance party!

They are jamming to DJ Joy,

jumping up and down to the beat.

The rumble of the thunder

is the stomping of the angels' feet

as they dance the night away.

Above the clouds,

the angels in heaven are showing off their
fabulous dance moves for the paparazzi
as the cameras flash away. The angels even
have their very own selfie station!

The lightning, so bright

in the sky, is the flash of the many

cameras capturing the fun.

Above the clouds,

the angels in heaven are having a contest
to see who can tell the funniest joke.
The jokes make the angels laugh so hard
they start to cry.

The raindrops

you see are happy tears of laughter.

Above the clouds,

the angels in heaven are having a race to see

who gets to be your guardian angel.

The lucky winner will get to be

with you always and forever!

The whistling of the wind

is the fluttering of the angels' wings

as they race as fast as they can.

Now that you know

what's really happening in heaven during a

thunderstorm, just imagine all the fun

the angels are having

above the clouds!

About the Illustrator

Kelly Mengarelli is an American artist and illustrator who illustrated *Princess Pippa and the Crown of Kindness*. Ever since childhood, she has had a passion for art, creativity, and imagination. Kelly graduated from Northern Arizona University, earning a Bachelor of Science Degree in Entrepreneurship, and turned her dreams of becoming a full-time artist into a reality. As a self-taught artist with no formal training, Kelly has the natural ability to make imagination come to life in the most whimsical way. She loves to add hidden details into every page so that story time becomes a more magical and interactive experience. Kelly's inspiration comes from color, beauty, fashion, and design. Her nickname, "The Artsy Blonde," most well suits her for her creative  and fun personality. Kelly lives in Arizona with her husband, where they both enjoy the outdoors, desert landscape, and spending time with family.

About the Authors

From left to right: Sue Milon, Carley Barton, and Stephanie Barton.

Sue Milon grew up in Lake Forest, Illinois and was always in trouble for staying inside and reading instead of being outside playing. At the age of 15, she knew she wanted to be a children's librarian and got her first job at the Lake Forest Public Library. After working as a bank teller, a secretary and a public relations librarian, Sue had "the best job ever" as an elementary and middle school librarian for 23 years in Runnemede, New Jersey. Sue lives up in the mountains in Prescott, Arizona with her husband, Dick, where they enjoy volunteering for various organizations. Sue and Dick have three grown children and eight amazing grandchildren. Her beloved stuffed animal, Lavvy, has been all over the world with her and never dreamt she would be included in a book!

Carley Barton was born in Dallas, Texas. As a child she was always adventurous and had no fears. She'd be yelling, "I'm OK!" as she was falling to the ground after a stunt and would always get back up again. Now she is an active high school honors student in Phoenix, Arizona. Her hobbies include photography, playing guitar, and taking care of her bearded dragon, Leo. Carley's an avid runner and her love of track inspired the ending to this book!

Stephanie Barton spent her childhood years in southern New Jersey enjoying the sights of Philadelphia and the boardwalks and beaches at the Jersey Shore. She went on to college at Arizona State University where she earned a bachelor's degree in exercise science and met her husband Jason. After a move to Texas early in their marriage, Stephanie found herself caught in a terrifying Texas thunderstorm with her young daughter. The storm became the inspiration for *"Above the Clouds: What Really Happens in Heaven During a Thunderstorm."*

Writing *"Above the Clouds"* has been a unique adventure. However, in her "real life," Stephanie has two passions: being a mom to two wonderful children and working as an exercise physiologist. She gets tremendous joy helping individuals with heart and lung disease build their confidence and improve their quality of life. In her very spare time, she enjoys traveling, exercising and playing games with her family. She is the reigning champion of Candyland in her household. Stephanie, Jason, Carley, and Reece now reside in sunny and hot Phoenix, Arizona, thankful to be over 1000 miles away from any Texas thunderstorm!